Celebrations

Happy New Year!

Clara Coleman

FINKELSTEIN MEMORIAL LIBRARY
SPRING VALLEY, N.Y. 10977

PowerKiDS press.

New York

3 2191 00968 0223

Published in 2017 by The Rosen Publishing Group, Inc.
29 East 21st Street, New York, NY 10010

Copyright © 2017 by The Rosen Publishing Group, Inc.

All rights reserved. No part of this book may be reproduced in any form without permission in writing from the publisher, except by a reviewer.

First Edition

Managing Editor: Nathalie Beullens-Maoui
Editor: Melissa Raé Shofner
Book Design: Michael Flynn
Illustrator: Continuum Content Solutions

Cataloging-in-Publication Data

Names: Coleman, Clara.
Title: Happy New Year! / Clara Coleman.
Description: New York : PowerKids Press, 2017. | Series: Celebrations | Includes index.
Identifiers: ISBN 9781499426717 (pbk.) | ISBN 9781499429480 (library bound) | ISBN 9781499426724 (6 pack)
Subjects: LCSH: New Year–Juvenile literature.
Classification: LCC GT4905.C65 2017 | DDC 394.2614–dc23

Manufactured in the United States of America

CPSIA Compliance Information: Batch #BW17PK: For Further Information contact Rosen Publishing, New York, New York at 1-800-237-9932

Contents

It's almost midnight, and my family is having a party. 5 ... 4 ... 3 ... 2 ... 1 ... Happy New Year!

5

We celebrate New Year's Eve on December 31.

6

There are other New Year
celebrations, too.

Ana's family celebrates
Chinese New Year.

It's also called the Spring Festival,
and it lasts fifteen days!

Friends and family celebrate together.

There is even a dragon
dance parade.

11

In Thailand, Kris and his family celebrate Songkran.

The streets turn into a big
water party every April.

Diwali is the celebration of
a new year in India.

It's also called the Festival of Lights.

Hana's family decorates with bright patterns and lots of candles. They hope this will bring them good luck.

The Jewish New Year is
called Rosh Hashanah.

A ram's horn called a shofar is
blown at the beginning and end.

David and his family gather for meals and prayer. It's a very important holiday.

21

There are New Year's celebrations around the world. How does your family celebrate?

23

Words to Know

candle

parade

Index

OCT 0 2 2017